# Nasreddin the Psychologist

by
## Tom Greening, Ph.D.

Illustrated by
Linda Hawkins

PUBLISHED BY GARDEN WALL PUBLISHERS

Garden Wall Publishers
Sherman Oaks, California
www.kenrmac.com
kenmozo@kenrmac.com

Nasreddin The Psychologist



www.tomgreening.com
tgreening@saybrook.edu



Designed by Linda Hawkins & Ken Rubin

Illustrations by Linda Hawkins

ISBN: 978-0-9916298-0-0

Reading these very short stories is a waste of time.

That is why I have made them as short as possible.

On behalf of Nasreddin I apologize for writing them.

When you have finished reading them go seek
enlightenment somewhere else.

Or give up. Then you may attain enlightenment.

Tom Greening

# Foreword

Nasreddin is a teacher, savant, clown, jester, Zen master, guru, fool. He could be a cousin of Alfred E. Newman, whom you can visit in Mad Magazine, and Mark Twain, who wrote light-hearted commentary on human foibles.

Nasreddin Hoca or Nastradin Hoxha or Nastradini is a 13th Century historical figure of philosophy and humorous story telling. He is claimed by many cultures and ethnic groups but he is especially associated with Turkey. Each summer the "International Nasreddin Hodja Festival" is held in Ak ehir, Turkey.

Although Nasreddin (with his faithful donkey) first lived, taught, and made a fool of himself and others many years ago, his spirit lives today. He has come back to us because he sees how badly we need his idiot wisdom. He has become a psychotherapist, an ominous threat to troubled seekers, an embarrassment to the profession, and perhaps a source of unexpected enlightenment.

You can learn more about Nasreddin at:
http://en.wikipedia.org/wiki/Nasreddin

NASREDDIN

# Table of Contents

# How to Be a Fool

**Seeker:** I hear Tom Greening has compiled a book of stories about you. Should I buy and read it?

**Nasreddin:** Yes. Tom Greening is a fool.

**Seeker:** Then why should I buy his book?

**Nasreddin:** It will be good for you to read a book by a fool about a fool.

**Seeker:** Why is that?

**Nasreddin:** So you, too, can learn how to be a fool.

# Stupid Questions

**Seeker:** Where are you from, Nasreddin? Some say
Persia, some say Turkey.

**Nasreddin:** And some say I've been sent by the Devil.

**Seeker:** Why do they say that?

**Nasreddin:** Because I give stupid answers to stupid
questions.

# Cure?

A prospective patient asked Nasreddin: "Can I be cured?"

**Nasreddin asked:**  "Are you a ham or a tobacco leaf?"

**The man answered:**  "No, of course not. I am a human being!"

**Nasreddin replied:**  "Then you cannot be cured."

# Fear of Heights

A man consulted Nasreddin for help in overcoming his fear of heights.

Nasreddin took the man to a cliff and pushed him off.

As the man fell, he shouted to Nasreddin, "Why did you push me off the cliff?"

Nasreddin replied, "Soon you will no longer be afraid of heights."

# Health?

A man came to Nasreddin and said, I feel depressed, bored, weighed down.  Can psychotherapy help me?

**Nasreddin replied:**  Yes.

**The man asked:**  How much does it cost?

**Nasreddin answered:**  $100 per session.

**The man asked:**  Are you sure psychotherapy will lighten me up?

**Nasreddin replied:**  Yes. Psychotherapy will certainly lighten your wallet.

# Afraid of the Dark

**Man:** I am afraid of the dark. What should I do?

**Nasreddin counseled:** At night, when it is dark, turn on a light.

**Man:** But then it won't be dark.

**Nasreddin:** True, and you won't be afraid.

# Under Qualified

**A man came to Nasreddin and said:** I need vocational counseling.

**Nasreddin asked:** What kind of work do you do now?

**The man replied:** I am a vocational counselor.

**Nasreddin asked:** Why don't you counsel yourself?

**The Man:** I tried but failed.

**Nasreddin:** My advice is that you should find another profession.

# Deserving?

**Seeker:** I want to be happy and free.

**Nasreddin:** Who said you are not?

**Seeker:** I did. That's why I came to you.

**Nasreddin:** But I don't know you or whether you deserve to be happy and free.

**Seeker:** Now I feel worse.

**Nasreddin:** See what I mean? Apparently you do not deserve to be happy and free.

# Once is Enough

A man invited Nasreddin to join him in hunting for mushrooms and to show him which mushrooms are edible.

Nasreddin assured him that all mushrooms are edible.

"But," said the man, "my mother warned me that some mushrooms are deadly poisonous."

Nasreddin replied, "That is true. Although all mushrooms are edible, some can be eaten only once."

# Wise Wife

**Man:**  My wife doesn't love me.

**Nasreddin:**  Are you lovable?

**Man:**  I don't know.  I think I am.

**Nasreddin:**  Maybe your wife knows more than you.

# Untrained

**Man:** What kind of training do you have to have to be a psychotherapist?

**Nasreddin:** None.

**Man:** How can you be a therapist with no training?

**Nasreddin:** Easily, because I don't have to forget it when I'm talking to you.

# Climbing

A prospective patient asked Nasreddin, "I have low self-esteem. Can you help me?"

Nasreddin gave him a ladder and said, "Climb this."

The man asked, "How can that help?"

Nasreddin replied, "Climbing it will elevate you."

# Congratulations!

**Seeker:**  Can you help me?  I have low self-esteem.

**Nasreddin:**  Congratulations!.  You don't need my help.

**Seeker:**  Why do you congratulate me?

**Nasreddin:**  Because you are very reality-oriented.

**Seeker:**  What do you mean?

**Nasreddin:**  From observing your craven seeking,
    I conclude you aren't worth much, so I congratulate
    you on your accurate self-assessment.

# Only Once

**Man:** I have difficulty relating to other people. How often should I come to therapy?

**Nasreddin:** Only once.

**Man:** How can coming only once help me?

**Nasreddin:** Therapy will end your problems in relating to other people if you come only once and never leave.

Nasreddin The Psychologist
Closed

# The Meaning of Life

**Man:** What is the meaning of life?

**Nasreddin:** Buy my book and you will learn it.

**Man:** But I want you to tell me.

**Nasreddin:** If I do, you won't buy my book, and then my life will have less meaning.

# Hopeless

**Seeker:** I want to be enlightened like you.  Tell me how.

**Nasreddin:** Stop wanting.  Just be.

**Man:** That is exactly the state I hope to achieve.

**Nasreddin:** You want "not-wanting."  You are hopeless, because you hope.

# Nightmare

**Man:** I wake up at night screaming but I don't know what I am afraid of.

**Nasreddin:** Choose something to be afraid of.

**Man:** But then I'll still wake up screaming.

**Nasreddin:** True, but at least then you'll know why.

# Hoping

**Seeker:** What do you hope people will learn from reading your book?

**Nasreddin:** I hope they will learn that they can't learn from reading a book by a hopeless fool who still hopes.

# Fishing

**Seeker:** Mullah, why are you silent?  You look restless, bored.

**Nasreddin:** I'd rather be fishing than talking with you.

**Seeker:** That is insulting.  I am offended.

**Nasreddin:** That is why I'd rather be fishing.  When I don't talk to fish they don't get offended.

# Crazy

A troubled man consulted Nasreddin for help.

**Man:** My family wants to commit me to a mental hospital.

**Nasreddin:** Why?

**Man:** Because sometimes I act crazy.

**Nasreddin:** Don't do that.

**Man:** How can I help it?  I am crazy so I act crazy.

**Nasreddin:** Stop it.  It is okay to BE crazy, but just don't
ACT crazy.

# Surrender

**Man:** How can I achieve inner peace?

**Nasreddin:** Surrender to what is.

**Man:** But I don't like to lose.

**Nasreddin:** Then defeat what is.

# Child-Raising

**Father:**  My children don't love me.

**Nasreddin:**  Why should they?

**Father:**  They are my children. I raised them.

**Nasreddin:**  Apparently you raised them wrong.
  Apologize to them.

# What Kind of God?

**Sinner:**  I pray to God to make me a better person. But it doesn't work.  I still do bad things.  What should I do?

**Nasreddin:**  Maybe God doesn't want you to be a better person.

**Sinner:**  What kind of God is that?

**Nasreddin:**  Your kind of God.

Everywhere
Uptown
Downtown
Markets
Business
Midtown
Nowhere

# Nasreddin's Trip

Nasreddin went to the big city.  When he returned his friend asked:

**Friend:**  How did you like your trip to the big city?

**Nasreddin:**  I didn't like it.  I got lost.

**Friend:**  So, you are glad to be home?

**Nasreddin:**  Yes.  Now when I get lost, at least I know where I am.

# Asleep

**Insomniac:** I need a drug to help me sleep.

**Nasreddin:** You don't need such a drug—you are already asleep.

**Insomniac:** What do you mean?

**Nasreddin:** You are asleep, dreaming that you are awake and need a drug.

# Be Grateful

**Unhappy Husband:** My wife won't talk to me.

**Nasreddin:** Why is that a problem?

**Unhappy Husband:** How can I live in a marriage with a wife who won't talk to me?

**Nasreddin:** You should be grateful and thank your wife.

**Unhappy Husband:** Why?

**Nasreddin:** I know many husbands who wish their wives would not talk to them.

# Enlightened

**Man:** How can I tell when I am enlightened?

**Nasreddin:** Buy a large, heavy book. While reading it, stand on a scale and note how much you weigh. Then put the book down. You will then see that the scale shows you have become lighter.

# Pointless

**Friend to Nasreddin:** You once bragged that you were going to take a trip around the world. What happened?

**Nasreddin:** I realized there was no point to doing that. At the end of trip I'd be right here, but poorer.

# Aba Zaba

**Head of UN to Nasreddin:**  How can we create peace between the warring countries of Aba and Zaba?

**Nasreddin:** I will send a donkey from Aba to Zaba, and I will send a donkey from Zaba to Aba.  Soon each donkey will become the leader of the country he is in. Then the former Aba donkey will not want to attack Aba. And the former Zaba donkey will not want to attack Zaba.  Please give me $100 for the fund to purchase and ship the two donkeys.  You will then be listed as an "Honorary Donkey."

ABA
ZABA
ZABA
ABA
LEADER OF ABA
LEADER OF ZABA

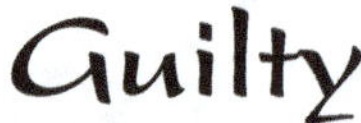

# Guilty

**Seeker:** I feel guilty that I don't love my parents.

**Nasreddin:** If you don't love your parents you are guilty.

**Seeker:** How is telling me that supposed to help me?

**Nasreddin:** Who told you that you deserve help?

# Not Me

**Nasreddin to visitor:**  Why have you come to see me?

**Visitor:**  I want to become enlightened, like you.

**Nasreddin:**  You can't.

**Visitor:**  Why do you say that?  You discourage me.

**Nasreddin:**  You are not me.  You can only become
enlightened like you.

# Childish?

A child came to see Nasreddin and complained: "My parents scold me and tell me to stop acting childish."

**Nasreddin:** But you are a child, so of course you act childish.

**Child:** Yes—and that is what they dislike.

**Nasreddin:** Tell them to replace you with an adult and to give you to someone who wants a child.

# Nasreddin's License

A bureaucrat came to Nasreddin and told him that  he must have a license to teach students.

Nasreddin showed the bureaucrat a license he had written for himself.

**Bureaucrat:**  That is not a valid license.

**Nasreddin:**  It is a valid license for a teacher who is not valid.

# Old Crow

One day Nasreddin climbed an avocado tree and began eating avocados.

The owner saw him and angrily asked, "What are you doing?"

Nasreddin replied, "I'm a hungry old crow eating lunch."

The owner demanded, "If you are a crow, show me you can fly."

Nasreddin jumped clumsily from the branch to one nearby.

The owner scoffed, "What kind of crow are you? That's not how crows fly."

Nasreddin replied, "That is how an old, hungry crow flies."

# Nasreddin's Donkey

Nasreddin ran low on money and could not afford to feed his donkey.  Fortunately, another donkey owner came to him for advice.

**Donkey owner:**  Mullah Nasreddin, I know you help humans, but can you help my donkey?

**Nasreddin:**  What is wrong with your donkey?

**Donkey owner:**  He is sad and won't eat or work.

**Nasreddin:**  I can't help you or your donkey.

**Donkey owner:**  Why not?  I thought you were a sage.

**Nasreddin:**  I am.  But I can't talk to a donkey.

**Donkey owner:**  Then what should I do?

**Nasreddin:**  Your donkey must tell his troubles to my donkey, not me.  But first you must give my donkey some hay.

# Compulsive

**Man:** Please help me.

**Nasreddin:** What is your problem?

**Man:** I have a hand-washing compulsion.

**Nasreddin:** But your hands appear to be dirty.

**Man:** I don't wash my hands. I wash other people's hands.

**Nasreddin:** That is not a problem.  That is a helpful service to others.  Here are a basin, water, soap and towel. Please wash my hands.

**Man:** No! I came here for psychotherapy.

**Nasreddin:** See!  Your compulsion is gone.

# Another Book

**Seeker to Nasreddin:**  Do you plan to make more of your stories available in another book such as this?

**Nasreddin:**  I'm not sure.

**Seeker:**  Why is that?

**Nasreddin:**  I will wait to see if this book saves the human race from itself.  If it doesn't, I will have to publish a sequel.

# Nasreddin's Car

Nasreddin bought a car with only three wheels.

A friend asked him why he bought such a car.

Nasreddin replied, "Gasoline is expensive.  This car will only cost ¾ as much to drive."

# Nasreddin on a Donkey

Nasreddin was sitting on a donkey facing backwards.

A student asked him why he was sitting that way.

Nasreddin replied, "The future is unknown and threatening.  The past has already happened and holds no upsetting surprises.  I find that view more appealing and less threatening."

# Blank Pages

A student saw Nasreddin studying a book with blank pages and asked him why he was doing that.

Nasreddin replied, "I and others have read many books with many words, and the human race does not get wiser.  So I decided to study just this one book with blank pages."

# Act the Fool

A villager asked Nasreddin, "Why do you act like a fool and say silly things?"

Nasreddin replied, "Out of courtesy and respect for my audience I speak in the language they can comprehend and I use simple vocabulary."

The villager protested, "Are you calling us fools?"

Nasreddin replied, "No. I am a fool for thinking you can understand me."

# Nasreddin's Dog

Nasreddin bought a dog as a pet.

The dog spent all its time sleeping or barking to be fed.

Nasreddin grew tired of this and reprimanded the dog.

The dog replied, "You knew I was a dog when you bought me.  Why are you complaining?"

Nasreddin was surprised, and said,  "Now that I realize you are a talking dog I will treat you nicer."

The dog replied, "I do not choose to talk to someone who was mean to me," and resumed barking.

At this, Nasreddin began barking.

# Nasreddin's Wisdom

**Student:**  If you are so wise, why do you spend your time riding around on a donkey telling stupid stories, instead of dealing with real life?

**Nasreddin:**  My wisdom consists of seeing and accepting that the present reality of human life on earth is simply not something that can be faced and endured.

# Sweet One

If reading these stories has not enlightened you, and even made you feel worse about yourself and life, consider this and the following stories:

Nasreddin came back from the marketplace with a basket full of hot chili peppers.  While he sat in his room eating one after the other, a student entered and inquired why he was eating what were obviously burning hot peppers.  Nasreddin's eyes were tearing, his lips were chapped, his nose was red, and his tongue was swollen inside his mouth.  "How can you do that to yourself?" asked the student.  "How can you continue to eat one awful pepper after another?"  Nasreddin replied, "I keep thinking that eventually I will find a sweet one."

# Stress Reduction

A troubled man asked Nasreddin: "Can you prescribe a
drug to relieve my stress?"

**Nasreddin:**  Yes. Cyanide.

**Man:**  Why cyanide?

**Nasreddin:**  You only need to take one dose, it is fast-
acting, it has only one side effect, and you will never
feel stress again.

# Nothing

**Seeker:** From all your years of helping people what is the most important lesson you have learned?

**Nasreddin:** Nothing.

**Seeker:** How tragic and stupid! Aren't you ashamed and disappointed?

**Nasreddin:** No. Learning nothing was enlightening.

# Again...and Again

**Seeker:**  I've read all your stories, but I am still not enlightened. Do you have anymore stories for me to read?

**Nasreddin:**  These are all the stories required for you to attain enlightenment. If you are still not enlightened go back and read them again…and again.

Plea

Alas, I've made a sordid scene
and need some help from Nasreddin.
I'm sure that he can fix my flaws
and get my crazy brain to pause
a little while so I can be
freed from my mind's insanity.
But if he can't, here is my plea:
just make me quite as mad as he.

Tom Greening

Nasreddin
the
Psychologist

by Tom Greening, Ph.D.

# The End

www.ingramcontent.com/pod-product-compliance
Lightning Source LLC
Chambersburg PA
CBHW082103090726
47910CB00008B/2577